COME OUT TO PLAY

by Jeanette Winter

Alfred A. Knopf ❧ New York

also by Jeanette Winter

HUSH LITTLE BABY

THE GIRL AND THE MOON MAN

This is a Borzoi Book published by Alfred A. Knopf, Inc.

Illustrations copyright © 1986 by Jeanette Winter.

2   4   6   8   10   9   7   5   3   1

Calligraphy by Carole Lowenstein

Library of Congress Cataloging in Publication Data

Winter, Jeanette. Come out to play.

Summary: Presents the Mother Goose rhyme inviting girls and boys to leave supper
and sleep and come out to play in the street by the light of the moon.
1. Nursery rhymes. 2. Children's poetry. [1. Nursery rhymes] I. Title.
PZ8.3.W725Co   1986   398'.8   85-5781
ISBN: 0-394-87742-X (trade); 0-394-97742-4 (lib. bdg.)

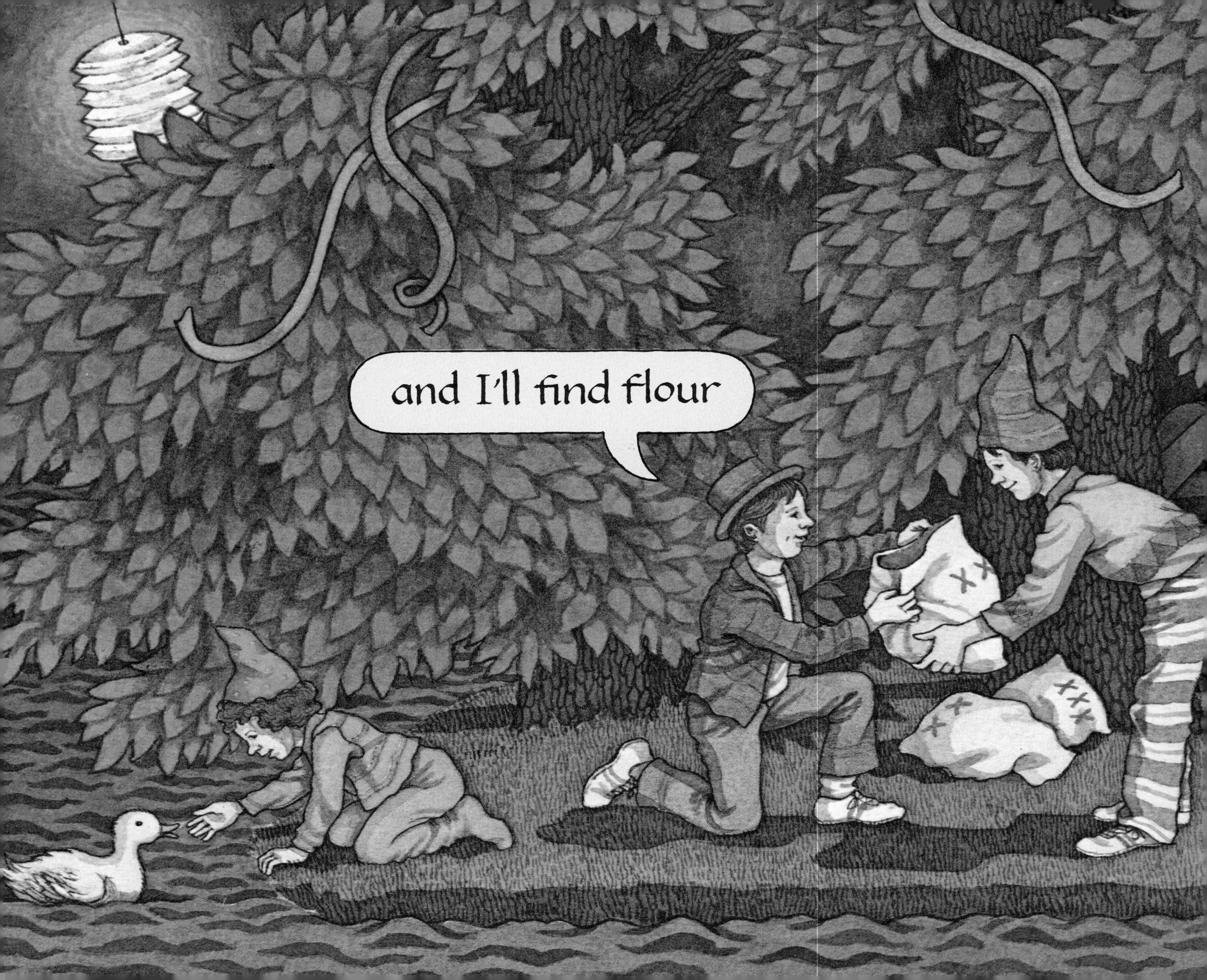
and I'll find flour

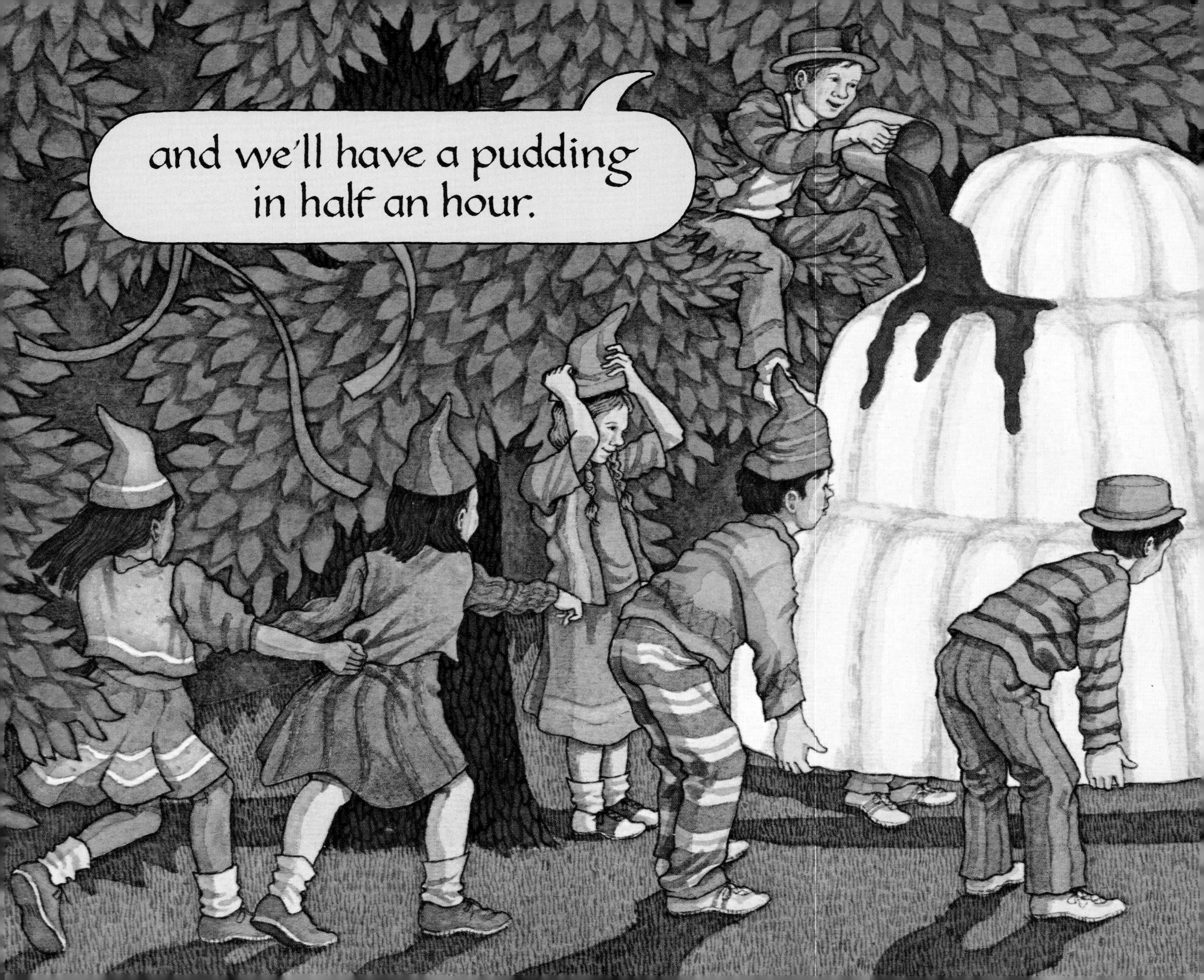
and we'll have a pudding in half an hour.

THIS BOOK BELONGS TO

C.C.N.S